Kes Gray

Mum and Dad Glue

Illustrated by

Lee Wildish

h
Hodder
Children's
Books

A division of Hachette Children's Books

My mum and dad are broken,
I don't know what to do.

My mum and dad have come undone,
I need to find some glue.

I need a pot of parent glue
To stick them back together.

I need to patch their marriage up,
I need to make them better.

I need to stick their smiles back on,
I need to get them mended.

I need them to be mum and dad,
The way they were intended.

They used to kiss
and cuddle,
But now they tut
and sigh.

They're breaking up.
    They're breaking up.

Am
I
the
reason
why?

They both say don't be silly,
That no one is to blame.

Although it's not worked out for them,
They love me just the same.

My friends say not to worry,
My friends say I'll be fine.

Lots of parents separate,

But
no,
no,
no!
Not
mine!

I need a pot of parent glue,
I need to find some fast.

I need to make them whole again,
I need to make them last.

I'm standing in the glue shop,
As far as I can see,

There's every glue that you could want,
Unless that you is me.

There's glue for model aeroplanes,

There's glue for plates and drawers.

There's glue for paper, glue for wood,

There's glue for tiles and floors.

There's super fast and super strong,

There's tubes and pots and tins.

Where every row of wrong glue starts,
Another one begins.

The owner of the glue shop
Asks what my glue is for.

And when she hears my answer
She softly shuts the door.

She puts her arm around me
And says it's time to see

That sometimes life works out this way,
That what must be must be.

I need to look beyond the break,
I need to think ahead.

I need to see that families
Can live apart instead.

The more I hold together
The more I'm super strong,

The more I'll come
to terms with things,
The less it will seem wrong.

Their love for me will never break,
It's chip and shatter free.

It also comes with something else,
A life-time guarantee.

We will love you forever
We will love you forever
We will love you forever
We will love you forever
We will love you forever
We will love you forever

I thank her for her kindness
And turn towards the door.

I wave to the adhesives
And leave with so much more.

If mum and dad could mend themselves
They would have done by now.

The will, the should, the must is there.
What's missing is the how.

Yes I have been hurting,
Yes it feels unfair.

But sometimes love gets damaged,
Way beyond repair.

I pull my life together
And smile as I depart.

I need to make the best of things,
There is no glue for hearts.

To everyone at Gingerbread

K.G.

For Laura, Grace and Oscar for being so patient x

L.W.

First published in hardback 2009 by Hodder Children's Books

Text copyright © Kes Gray 2009
Illustration copyright © Lee Wildish 2009

Hodder Children's Books
338 Euston Road, London NW1 3BH

Hodder Children's Books Australia
Level 17/207 Kent Street, Sydney, NSW 2000

A catalogue record of this book is available from the British Library.

ISBN: 978 0 340 95710 3
10 9 8 7 6 5 4 3 2 1

Printed in China

Hodder Children's Books is a division of Hachette Children's Books,
an Hachette UK Company
www.hachette.co.uk